THE SUPER SPEEDY MART

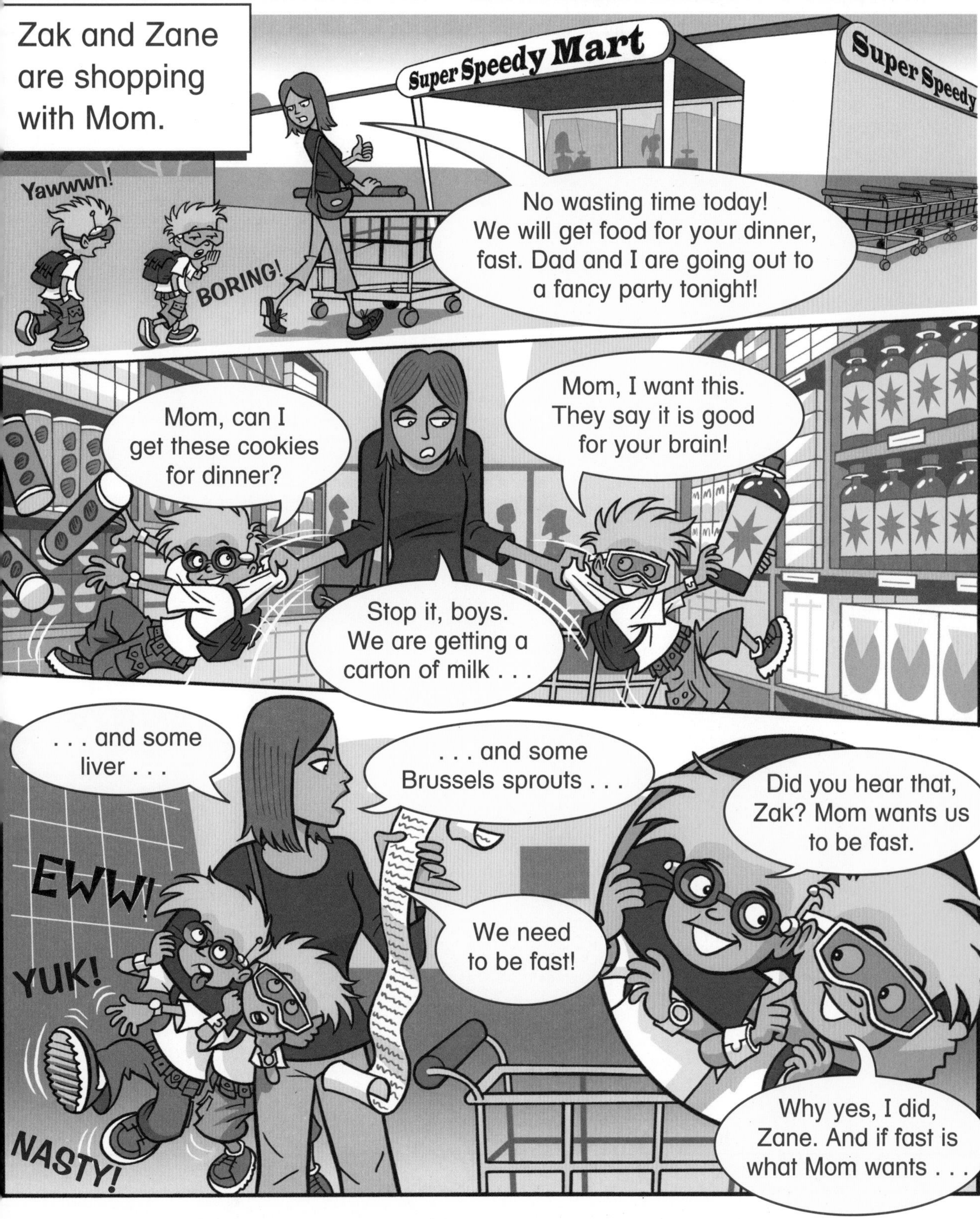
Zak and Zane are shopping with Mom.
Super Speedy Mart
Super Speedy
Yawwwn!
BORING!
No wasting time today! We will get food for your dinner, fast. Dad and I are going out to a fancy party tonight!
Mom, can I get these cookies for dinner?
Mom, I want this. They say it is good for your brain!
Stop it, boys. We are getting a carton of milk . . .
. . . and some liver . . .
. . . and some Brussels sprouts . . .
We need to be fast!
EWW!
YUK!
NASTY!
Did you hear that, Zak? Mom wants us to be fast.
Why yes, I did, Zane. And if fast is what Mom wants . . .

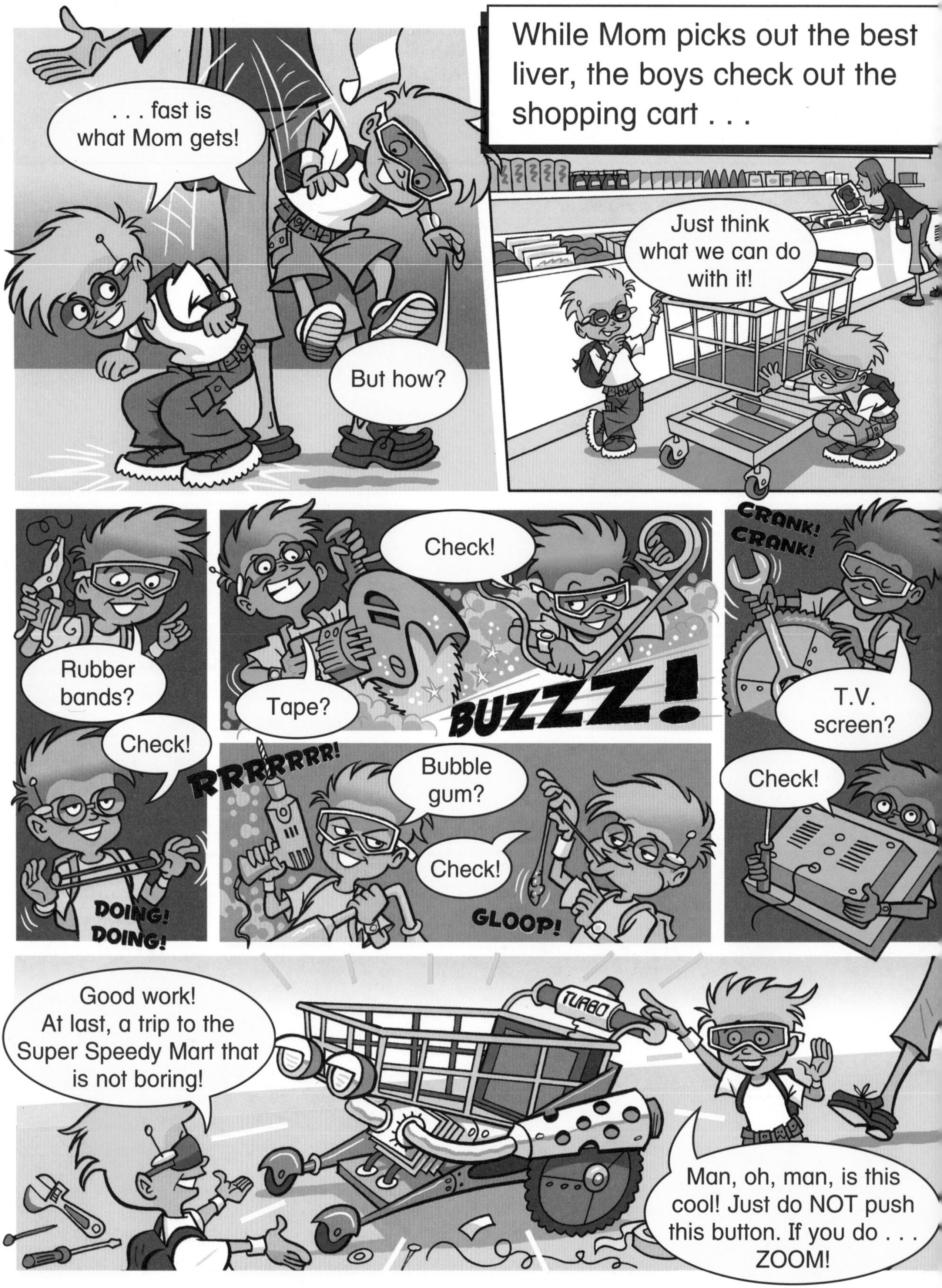

. . . fast is what Mom gets!
But how?
While Mom picks out the best liver, the boys check out the shopping cart . . .
Just think what we can do with it!
Rubber bands?
Check!
DOING! DOING!
Check!
Tape?
BUZZZ!
RRRRRRR!
Bubble gum?
Check!
GLOOP!
CRANK! CRANK!
T.V. screen?
Check!
Good work! At last, a trip to the Super Speedy Mart that is not boring!
TURBO
Man, oh, man, is this cool! Just do NOT push this button. If you do . . . ZOOM!

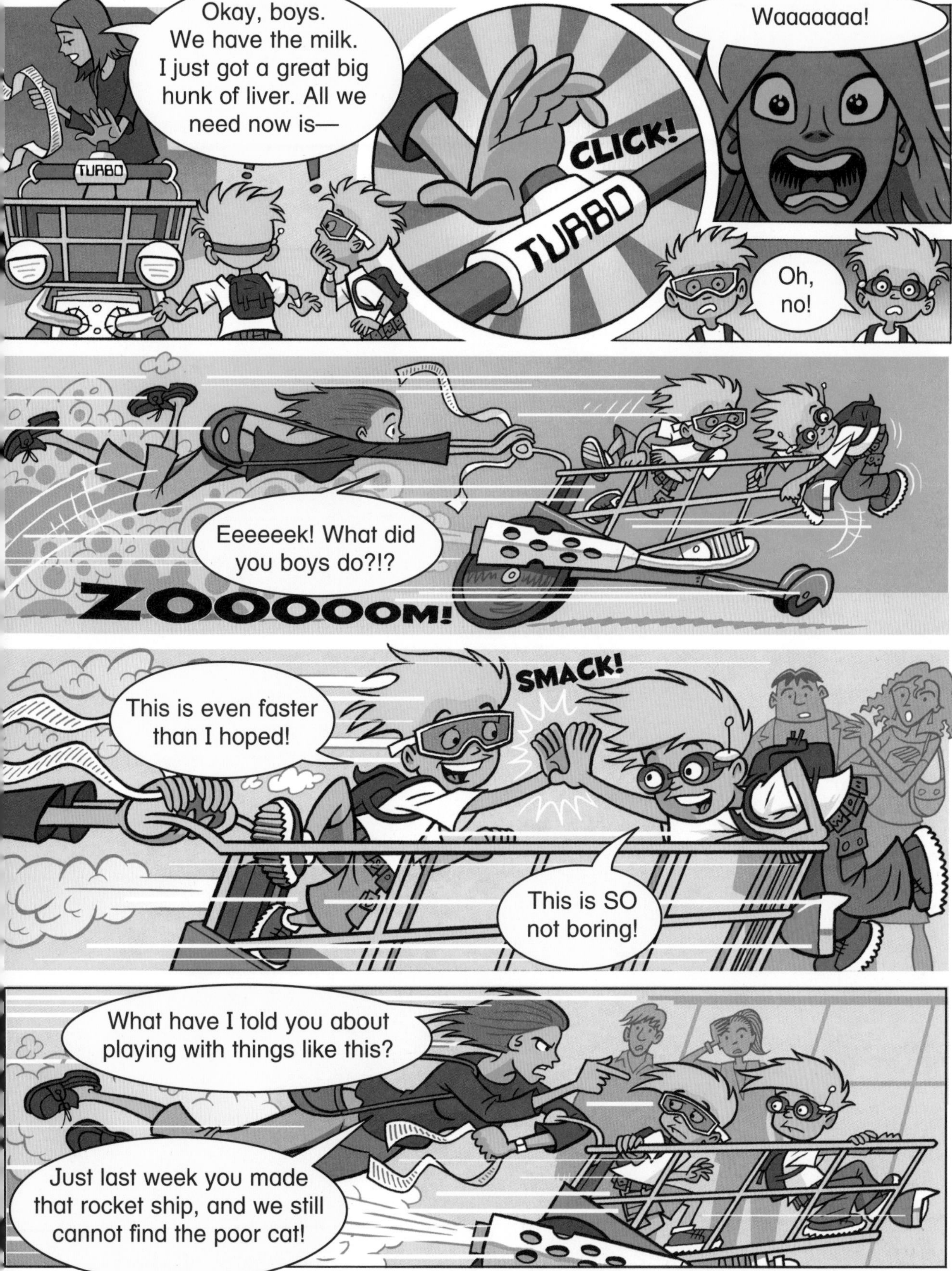
Okay, boys. We have the milk. I just got a great big hunk of liver. All we need now is—
TURBO
CLICK!
TURBO
Waaaaaaa!
Oh, no!
Eeeeeek! What did you boys do?!?
ZOOOOOOM!
This is even faster than I hoped!
SMACK!
This is SO not boring!
What have I told you about playing with things like this?
Just last week you made that rocket ship, and we still cannot find the poor cat!

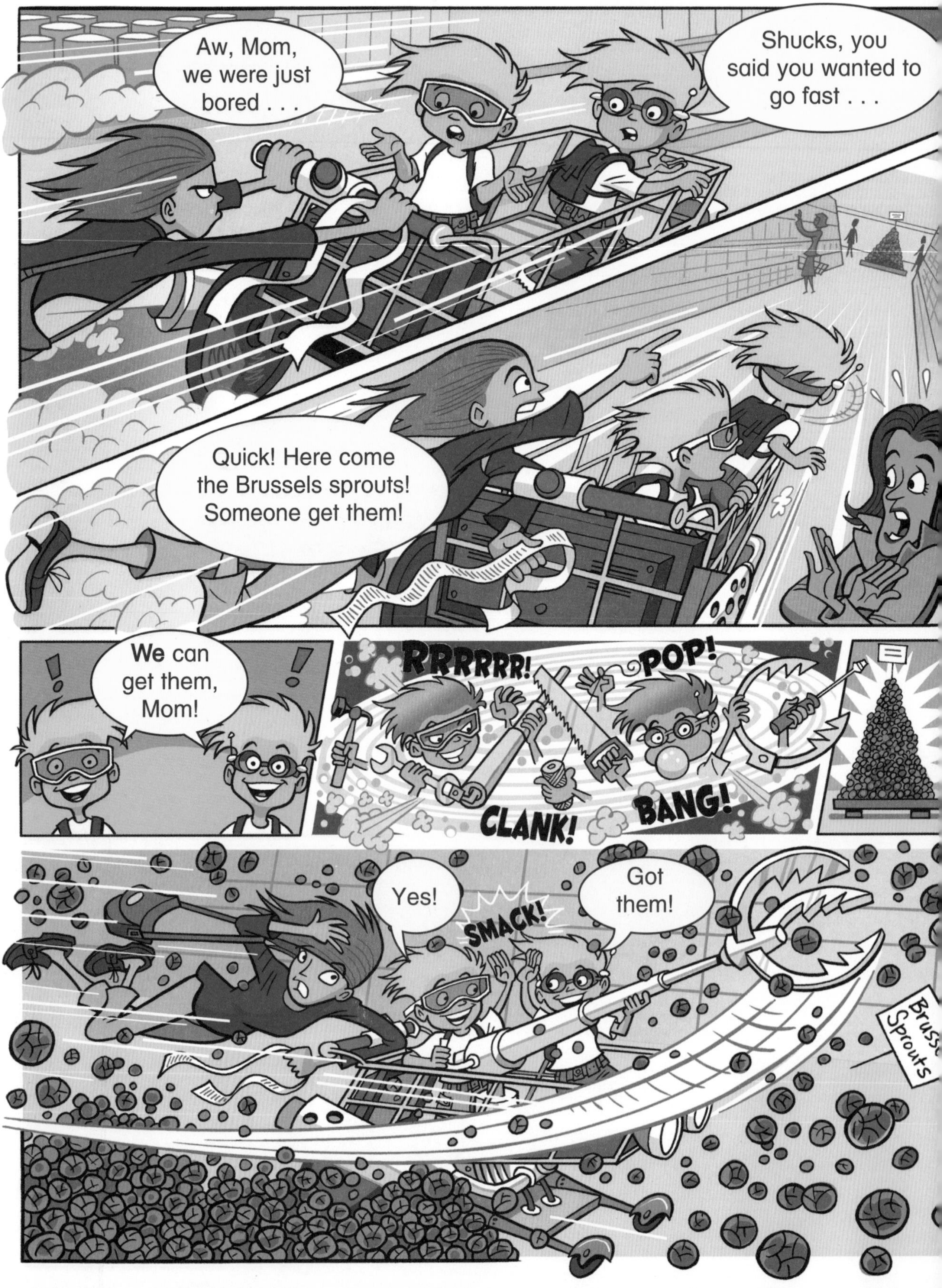
Aw, Mom, we were just bored . . .
Shucks, you said you wanted to go fast . . .
Quick! Here come the Brussels sprouts! Someone get them!
We can get them, Mom!
RRRRRR!
POP!
CLANK!
BANG!
Yes!
SMACK!
Got them!
Bruss Sprouts

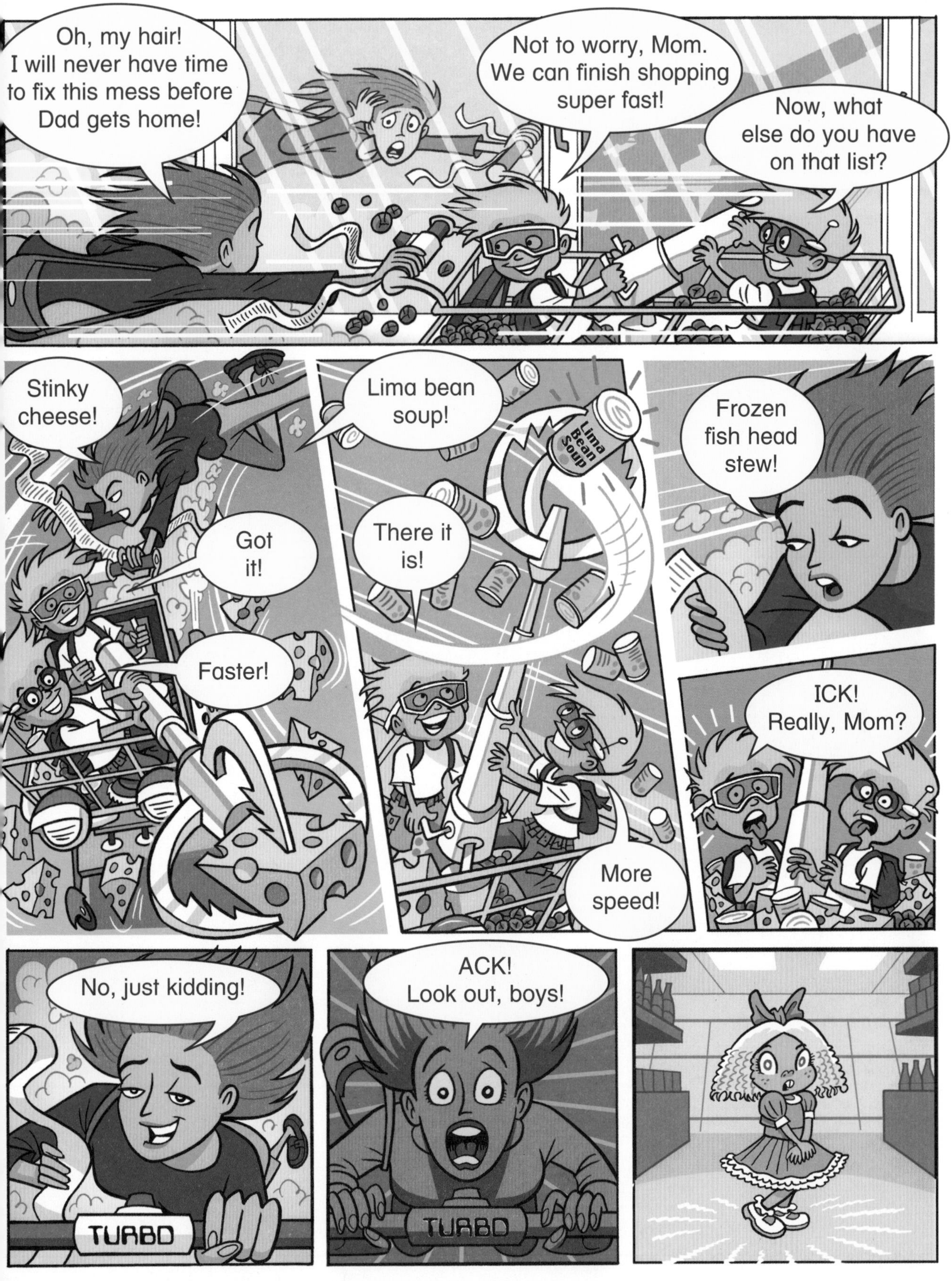
Oh, my hair! I will never have time to fix this mess before Dad gets home!
Not to worry, Mom. We can finish shopping super fast!
Now, what else do you have on that list?
Stinky cheese!
Got it!
Faster!
Lima bean soup!
Lima Bean Soup
There it is!
More speed!
Frozen fish head stew!
ICK! Really, Mom?
No, just kidding!
TURBO
ACK! Look out, boys!
TURBO

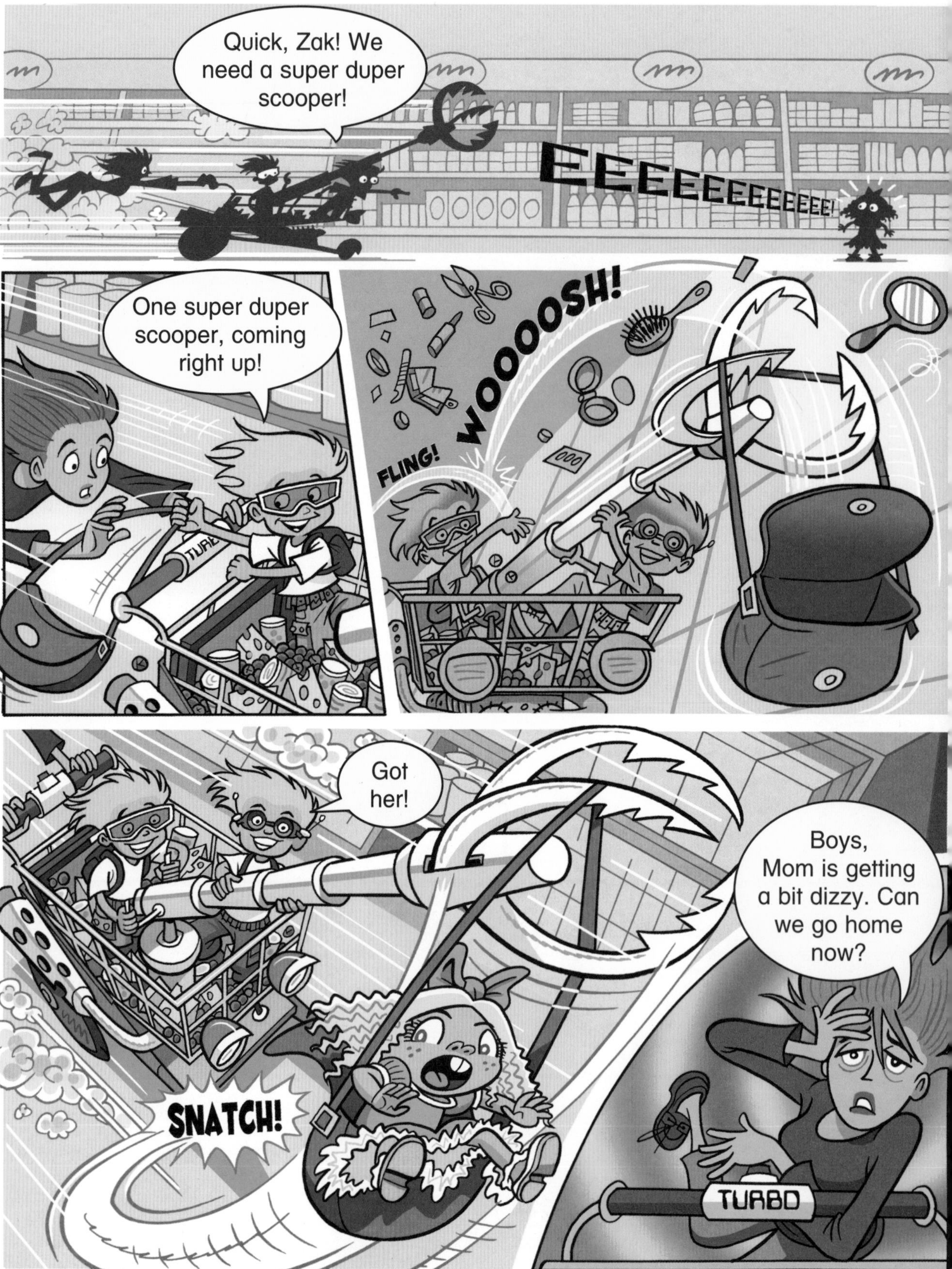

Quick, Zak! We need a super duper scooper!
EEEEEEEEEEEEE!
One super duper scooper, coming right up!
TURB
WOOOOSH!
FLING!
Got her!
SNATCH!
Boys, Mom is getting a bit dizzy. Can we go home now?
TURBO

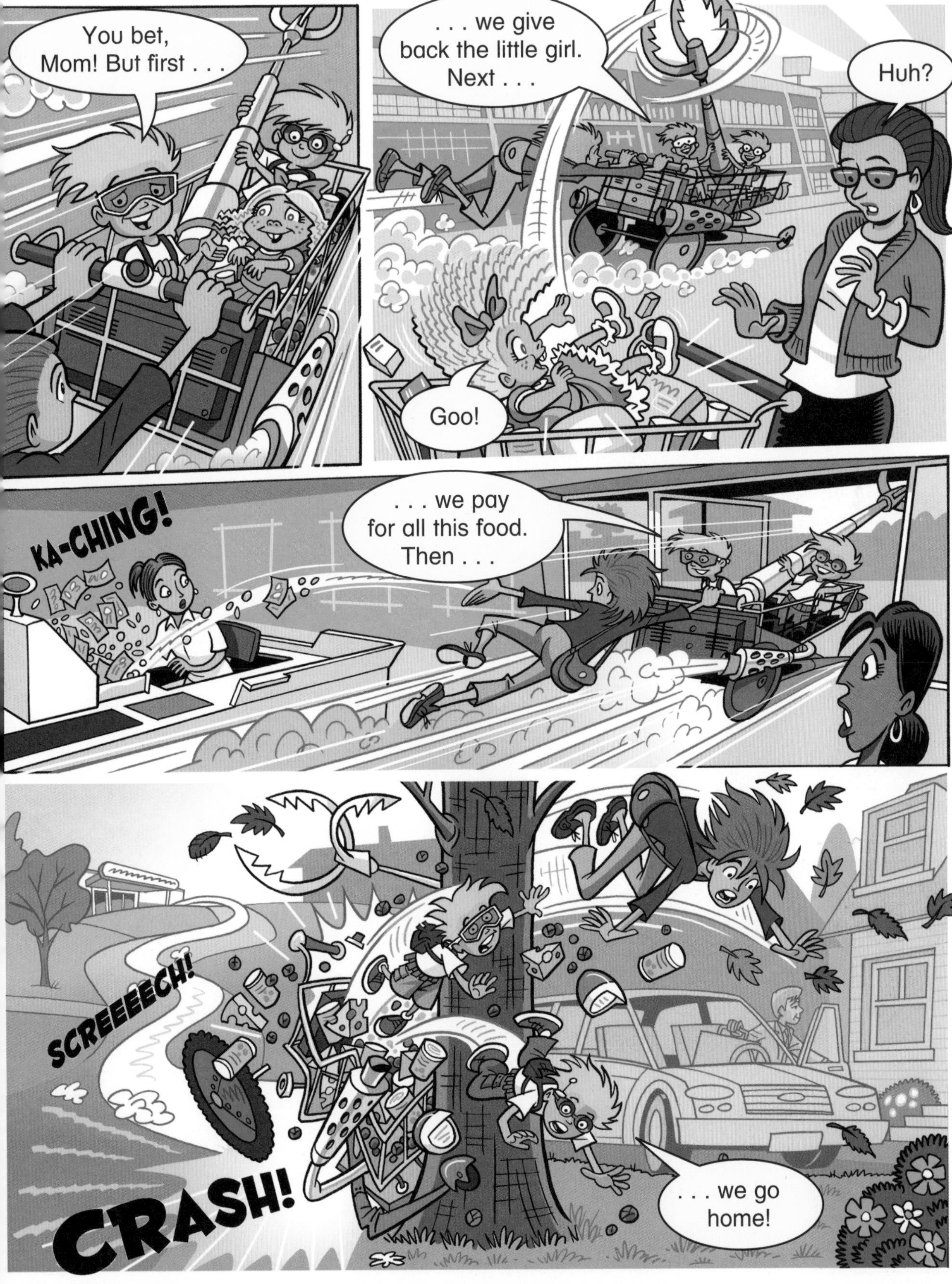
You bet, Mom! But first . . .
. . . we give back the little girl. Next . . .
Huh?
Goo!
KA-CHING!
. . . we pay for all this food. Then . . .
SCREEEEECH!
CRASH!
. . . we go home!

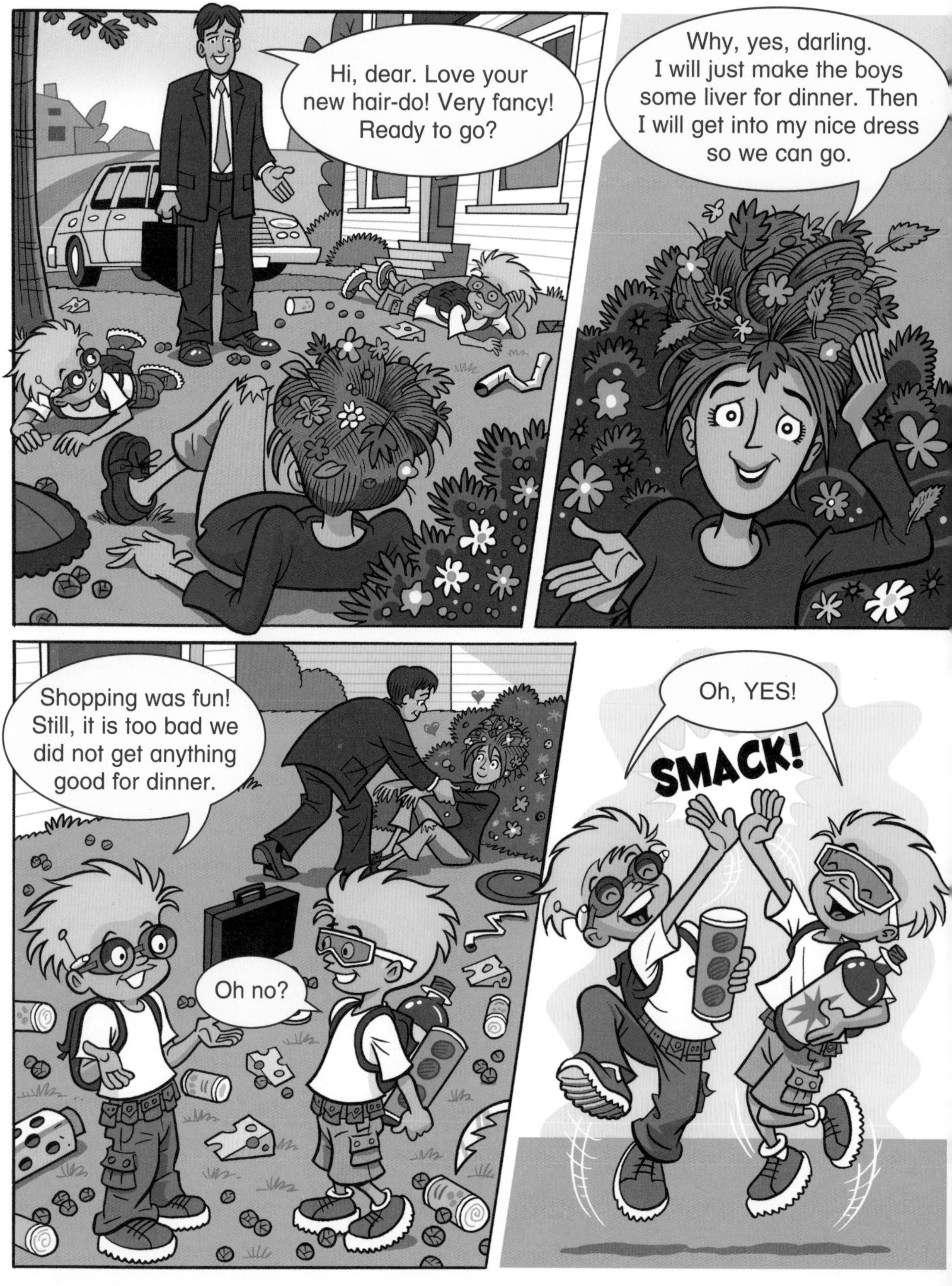
Hi, dear. Love your new hair-do! Very fancy! Ready to go?
Why, yes, darling. I will just make the boys some liver for dinner. Then I will get into my nice dress so we can go.
Shopping was fun! Still, it is too bad we did not get anything good for dinner.
Oh no?
Oh, YES!
SMACK!

SMALL WONDERS

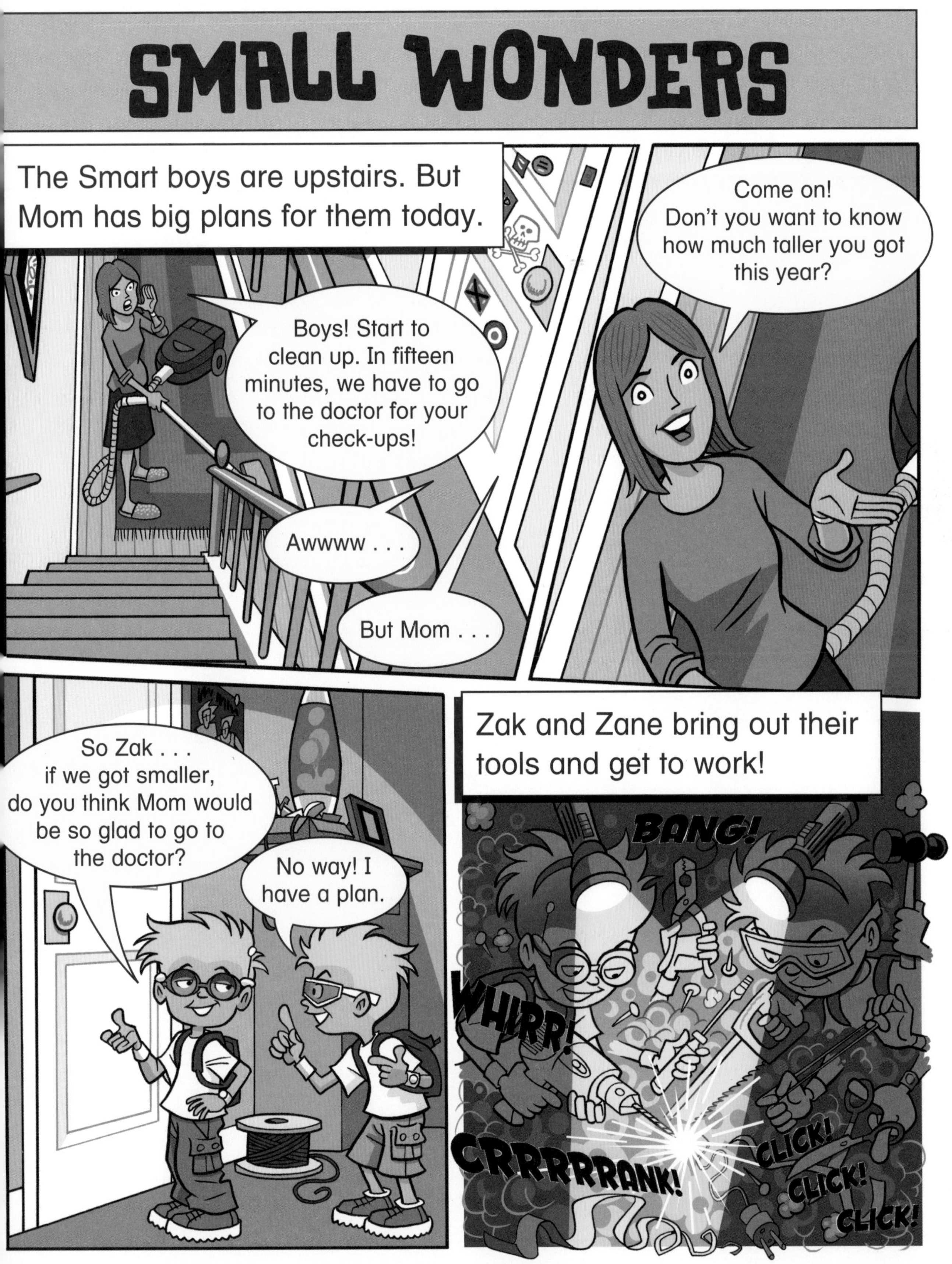
The Smart boys are upstairs. But Mom has big plans for them today.
Boys! Start to clean up. In fifteen minutes, we have to go to the doctor for your check-ups!
Awwww . . .
But Mom . . .
Come on! Don't you want to know how much taller you got this year?
So Zak . . . if we got smaller, do you think Mom would be so glad to go to the doctor?
No way! I have a plan.
Zak and Zane bring out their tools and get to work!
BANG!
WHIRR!
CRRRRRRANK!
CLICK!
CLICK!
CLICK!

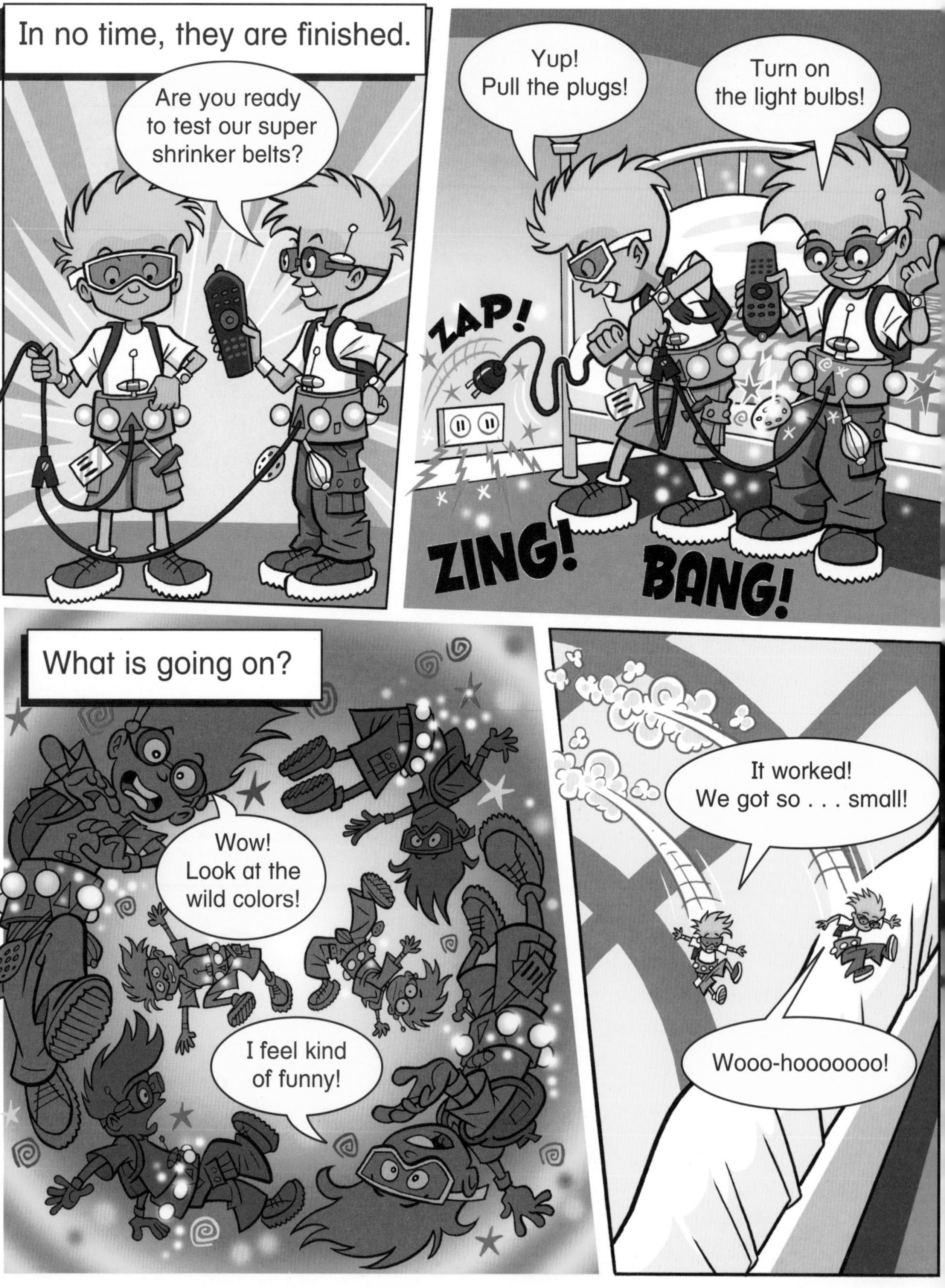
In no time, they are finished.
Are you ready to test our super shrinker belts?
Yup! Pull the plugs!
Turn on the light bulbs!
ZAP!
ZING!
BANG!
What is going on?
Wow! Look at the wild colors!
I feel kind of funny!
It worked! We got so . . . small!
Wooo-hooooooo!

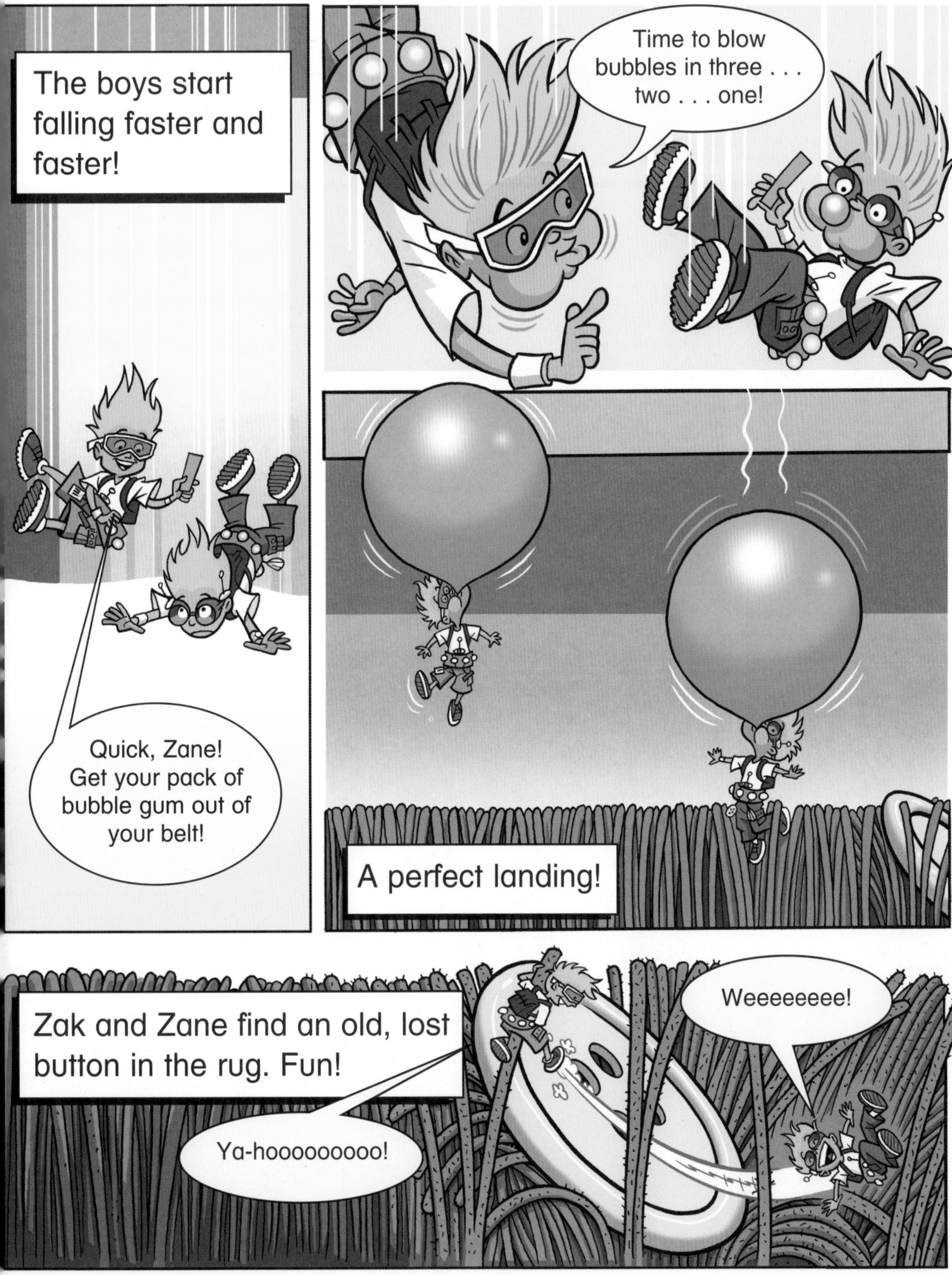
The boys start falling faster and faster!
Time to blow bubbles in three . . . two . . . one!
Quick, Zane! Get your pack of bubble gum out of your belt!
A perfect landing!
Zak and Zane find an old, lost button in the rug. Fun!
Weeeeeeee!
Ya-hooooooooo!

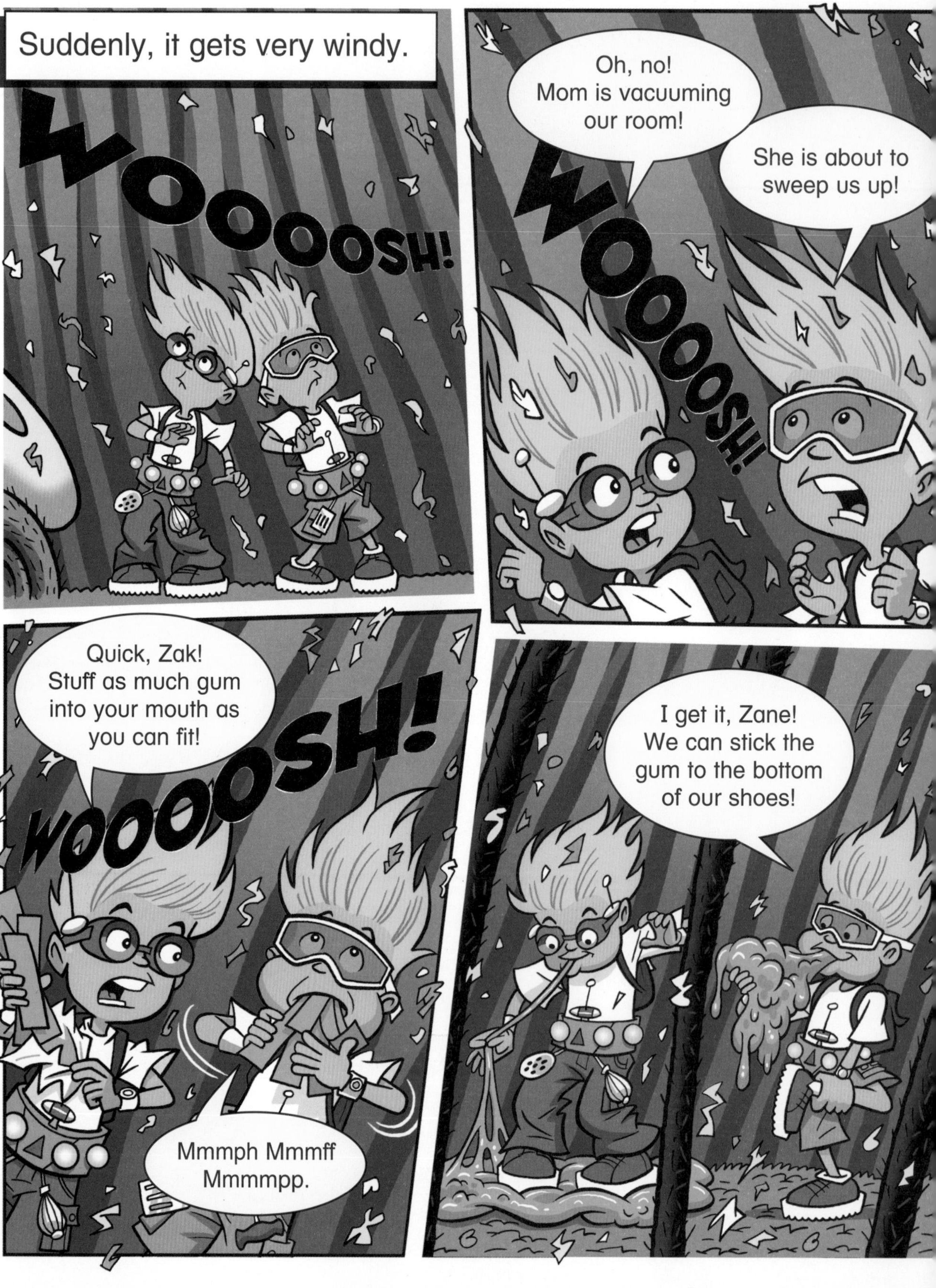
Suddenly, it gets very windy.
WOOOOOSH!
Oh, no!
Mom is vacuuming
our room!
She is about to
sweep us up!
WOOOOOSH!
Quick, Zak!
Stuff as much gum
into your mouth as
you can fit!
WOOOOSH!
Mmmph Mmmff
Mmmmpp.
I get it, Zane!
We can stick the
gum to the bottom
of our shoes!

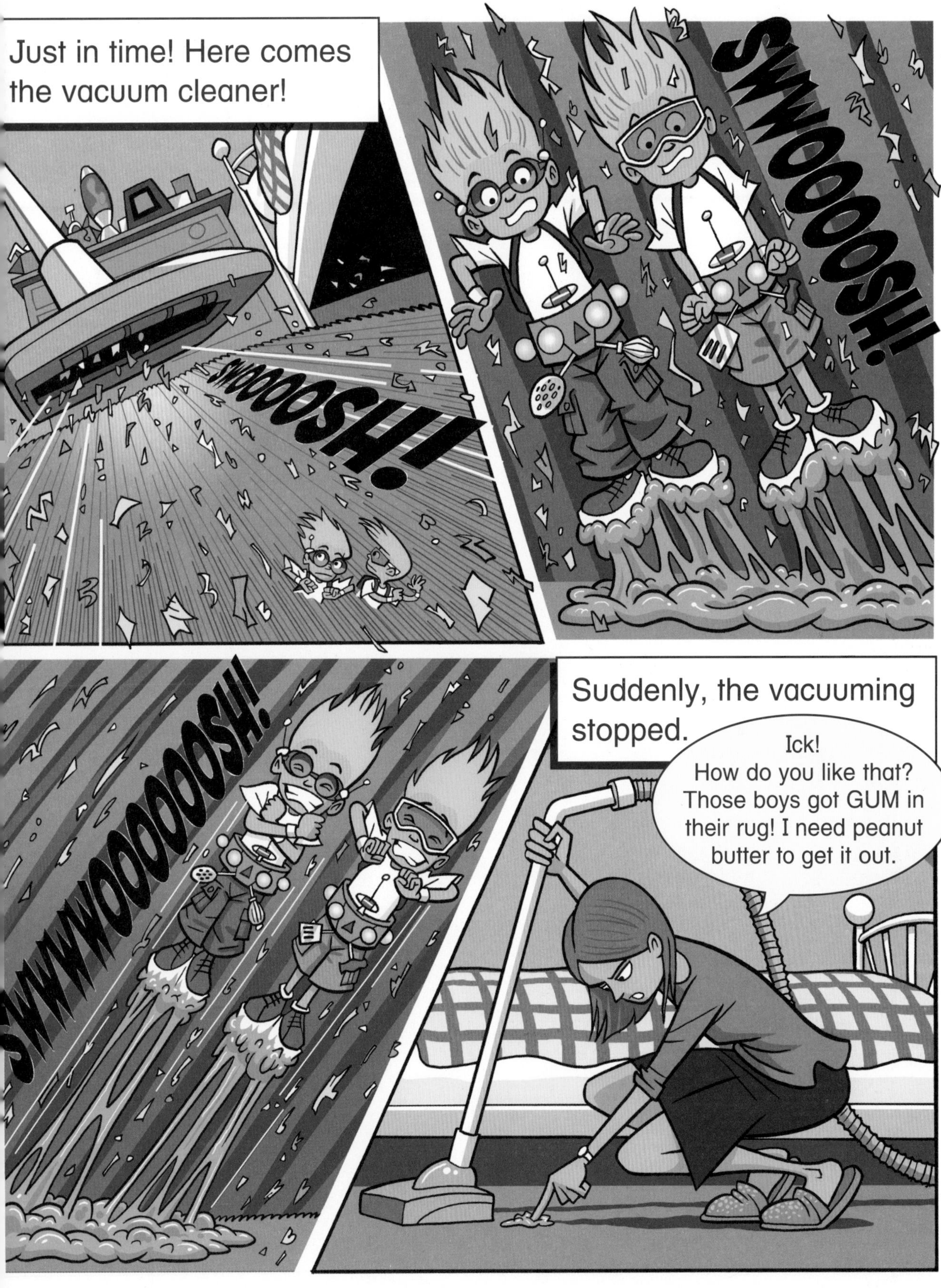
Just in time! Here comes the vacuum cleaner!
SWOOOOSH!
SWOOOOOSH!
SWWWOOOOOOSH!
Suddenly, the vacuuming stopped.
Ick! How do you like that? Those boys got GUM in their rug! I need peanut butter to get it out.

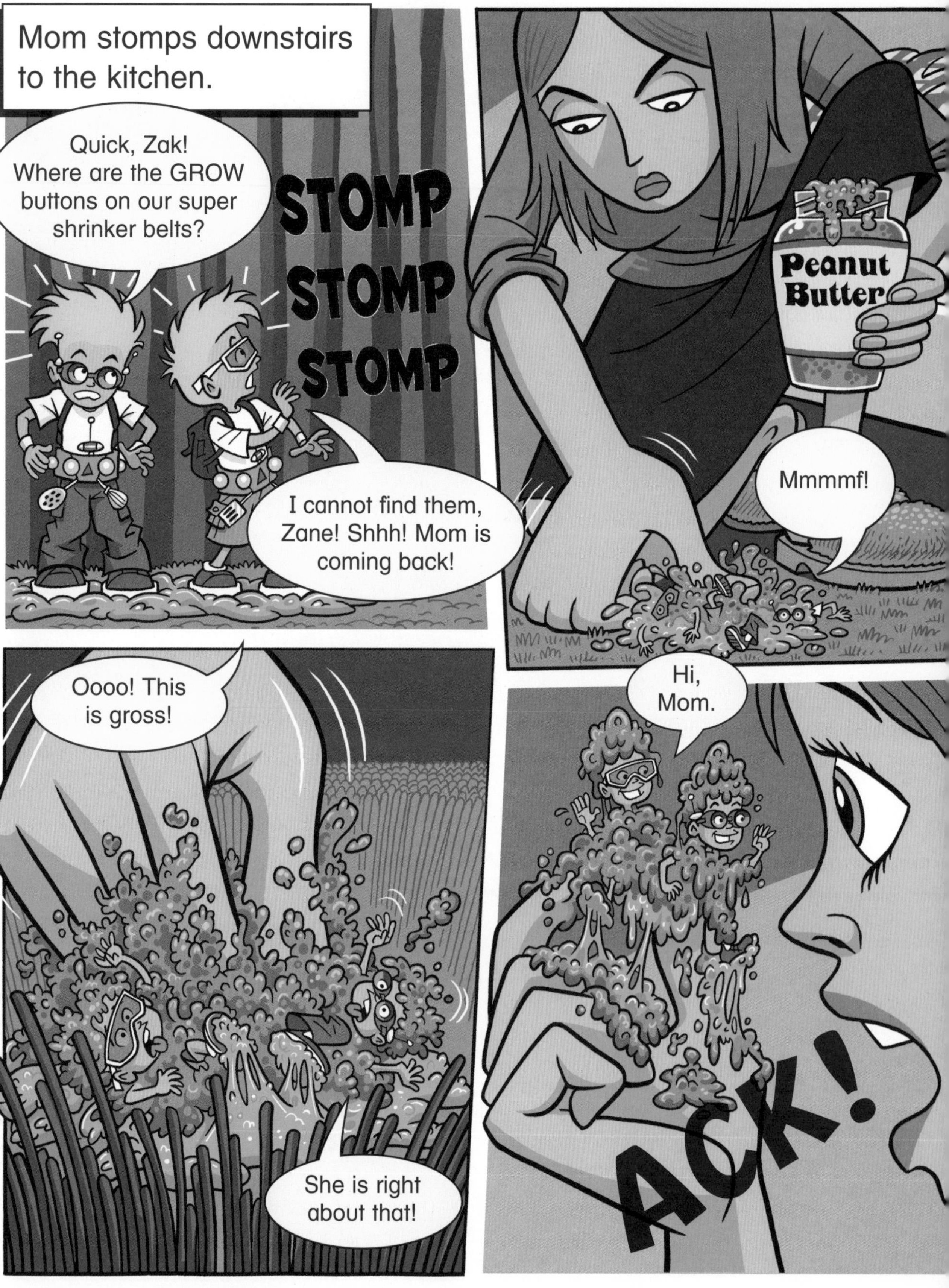
Mom stomps downstairs to the kitchen.
Quick, Zak! Where are the GROW buttons on our super shrinker belts?
STOMP
STOMP
STOMP
I cannot find them, Zane! Shhh! Mom is coming back!
Peanut Butter
Mmmmf!
Oooo! This is gross!
She is right about that!
Hi, Mom.
ACK!

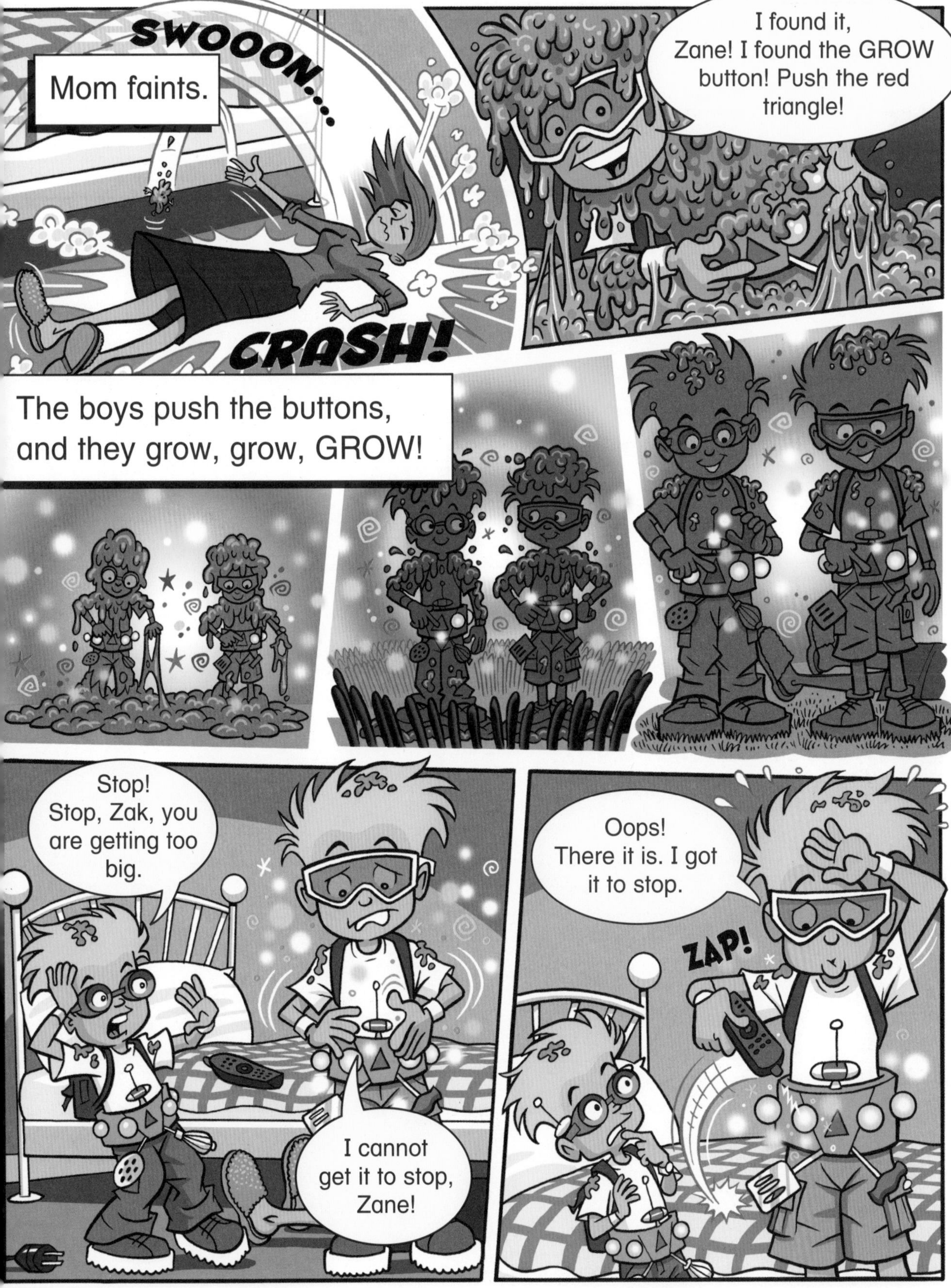
SWOOON....
Mom faints.
CRASH!
I found it, Zane! I found the GROW button! Push the red triangle!
The boys push the buttons, and they grow, grow, GROW!
Stop! Stop, Zak, you are getting too big.
I cannot get it to stop, Zane!
Oops! There it is. I got it to stop.
ZAP!

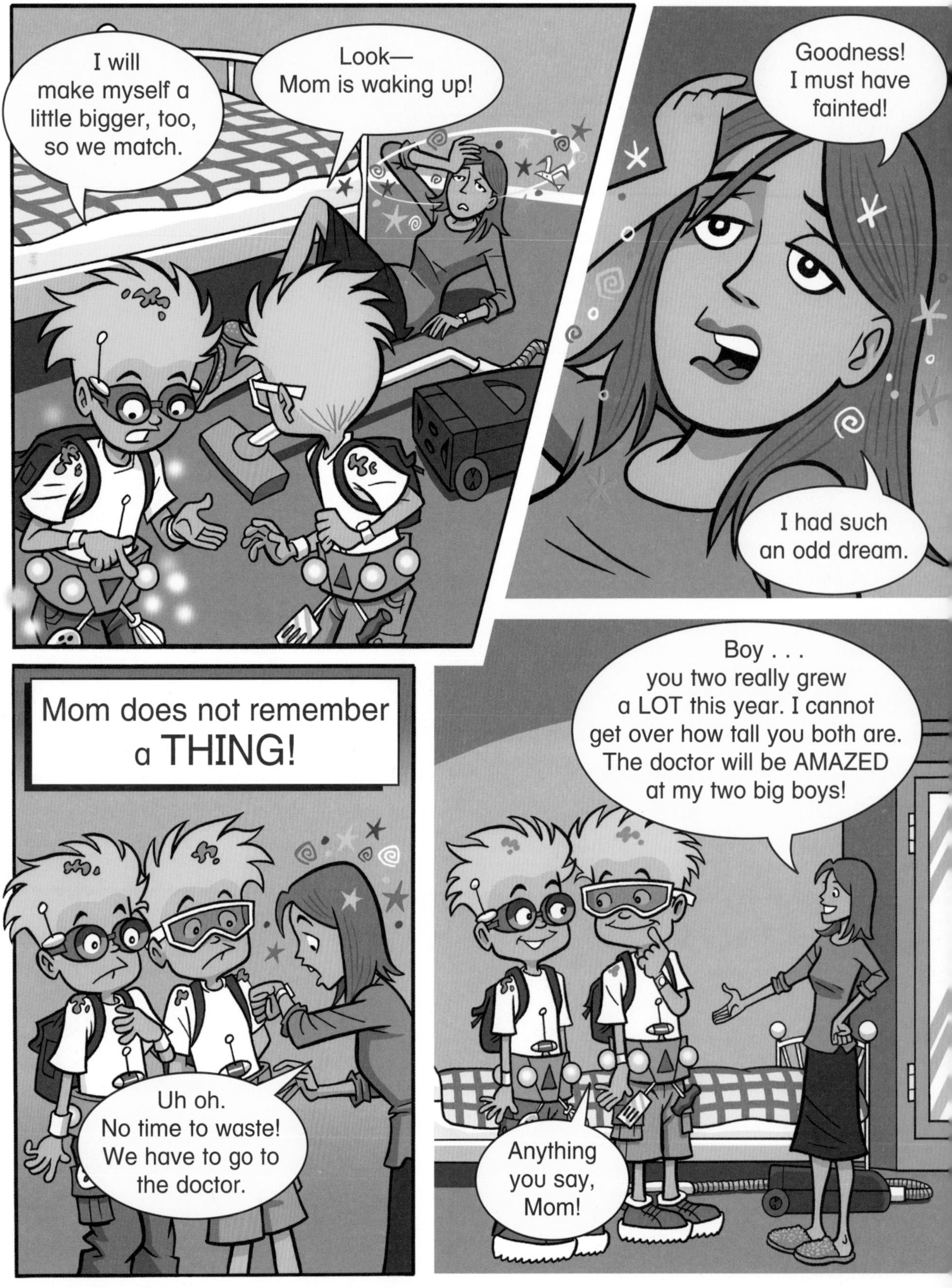
I will make myself a little bigger, too, so we match.
Look— Mom is waking up!
Goodness! I must have fainted!
I had such an odd dream.
Mom does not remember a THING!
Uh oh. No time to waste! We have to go to the doctor.
Boy . . . you two really grew a LOT this year. I cannot get over how tall you both are. The doctor will be AMAZED at my two big boys!
Anything you say, Mom!

Night and Day!

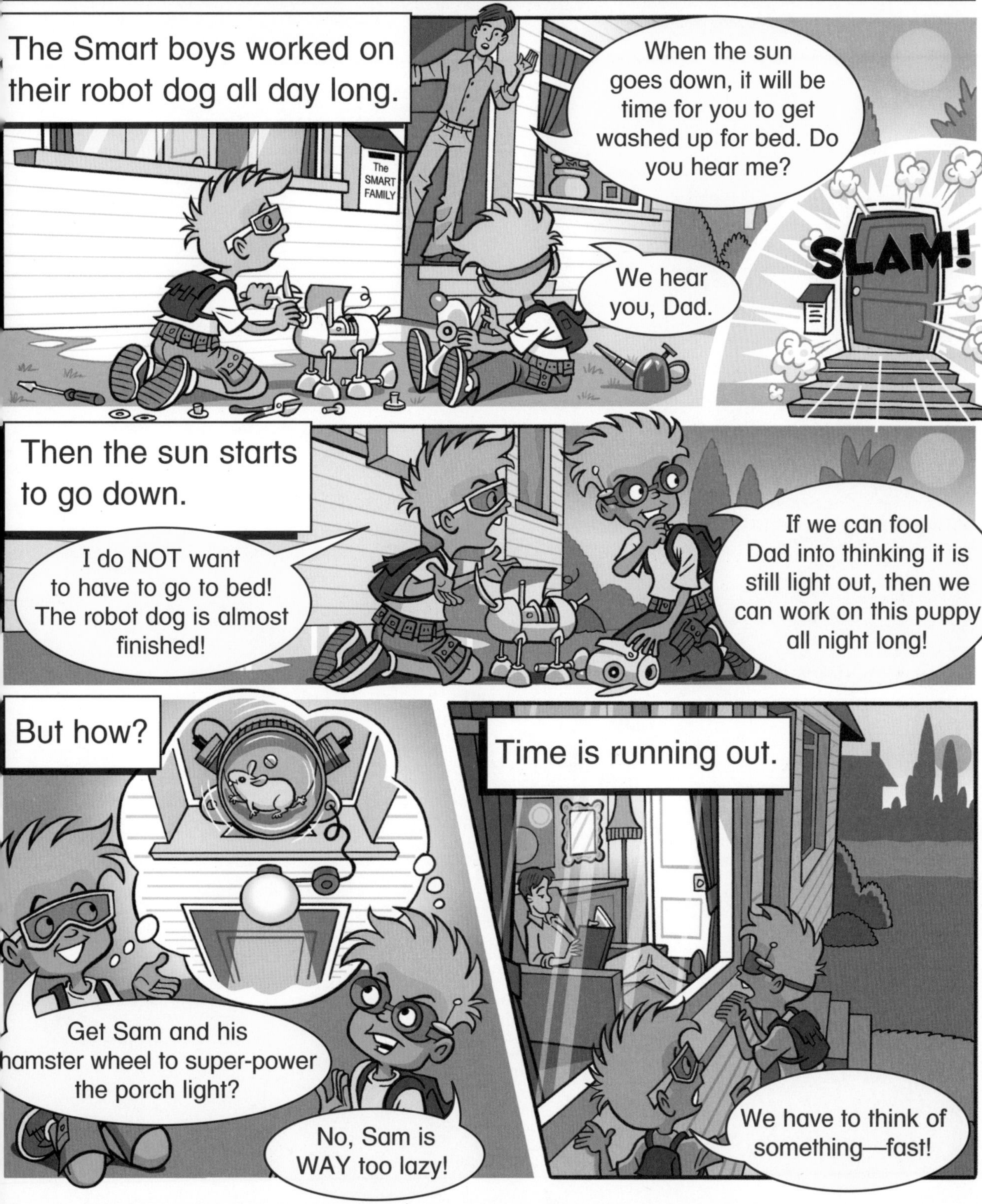
The Smart boys worked on their robot dog all day long.
The SMART FAMILY
When the sun goes down, it will be time for you to get washed up for bed. Do you hear me?
We hear you, Dad.
SLAM!
Then the sun starts to go down.
I do NOT want to have to go to bed! The robot dog is almost finished!
If we can fool Dad into thinking it is still light out, then we can work on this puppy all night long!
But how?
Get Sam and his hamster wheel to super-power the porch light?
No, Sam is WAY too lazy!
Time is running out.
We have to think of something—fast!

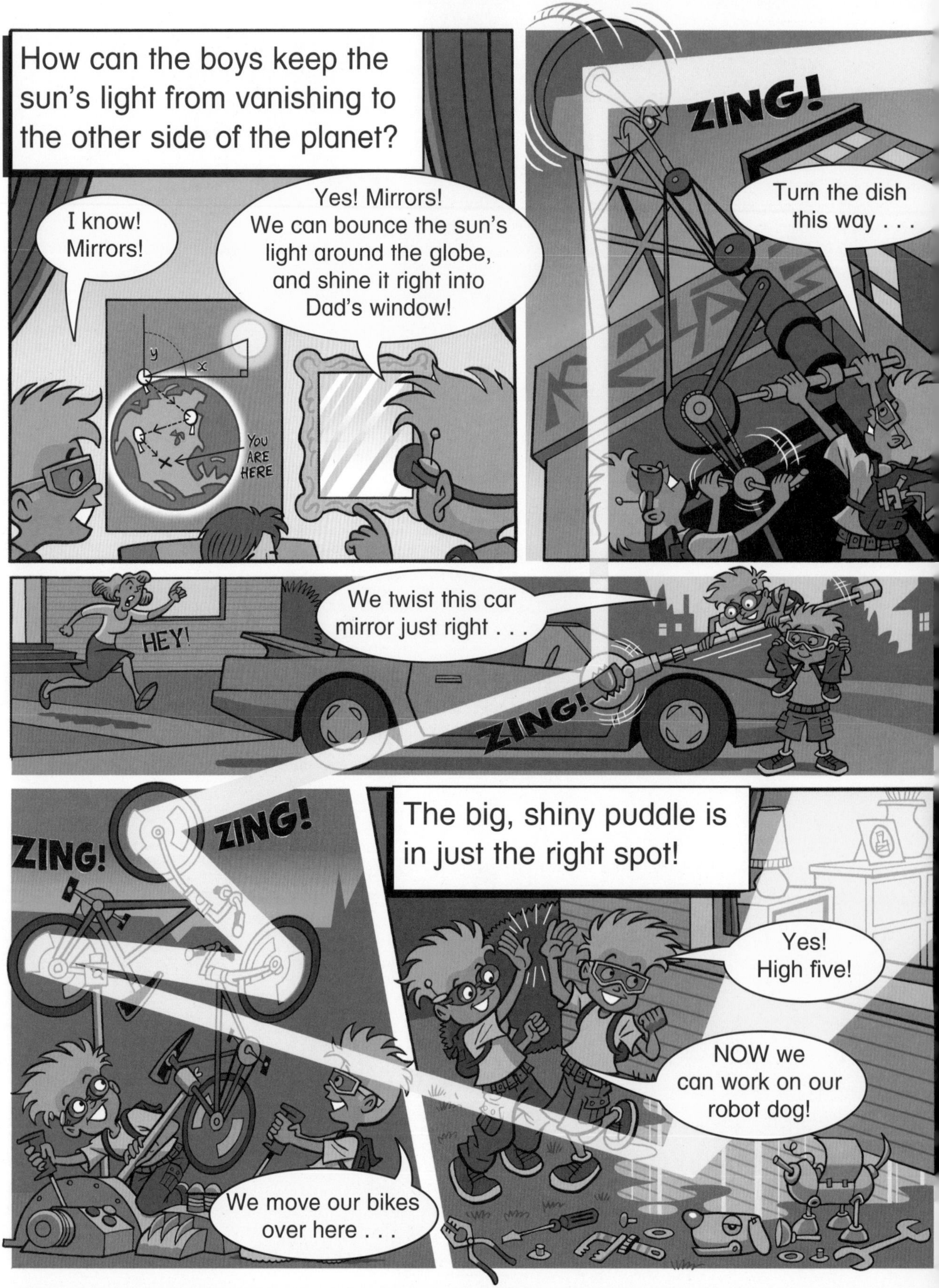
How can the boys keep the sun's light from vanishing to the other side of the planet?
I know! Mirrors!
Yes! Mirrors! We can bounce the sun's light around the globe, and shine it right into Dad's window!
y
x
YOU ARE HERE
ZING!
Turn the dish this way . . .
HEY!
We twist this car mirror just right . . .
ZING!
ZING!
ZING!
We move our bikes over here . . .
The big, shiny puddle is in just the right spot!
Yes! High five!
NOW we can work on our robot dog!

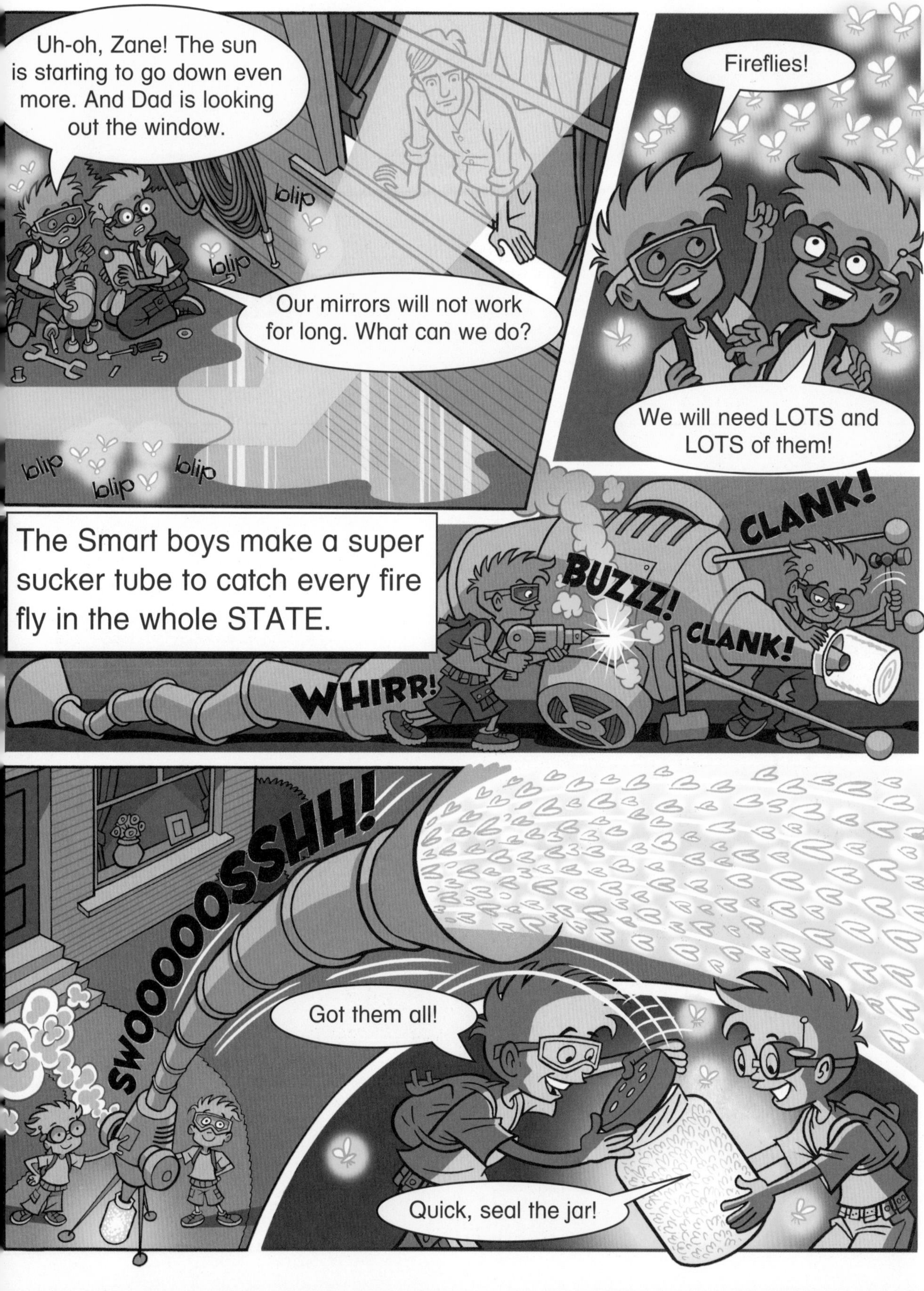
Uh-oh, Zane! The sun is starting to go down even more. And Dad is looking out the window.
blip
blip
Our mirrors will not work for long. What can we do?
blip
blip
blip
Fireflies!
We will need LOTS and LOTS of them!
The Smart boys make a super sucker tube to catch every fire fly in the whole STATE.
CLANK!
BUZZZ!
CLANK!
WHIRR!
SWOOOOOOSSHH!
Got them all!
Quick, seal the jar!

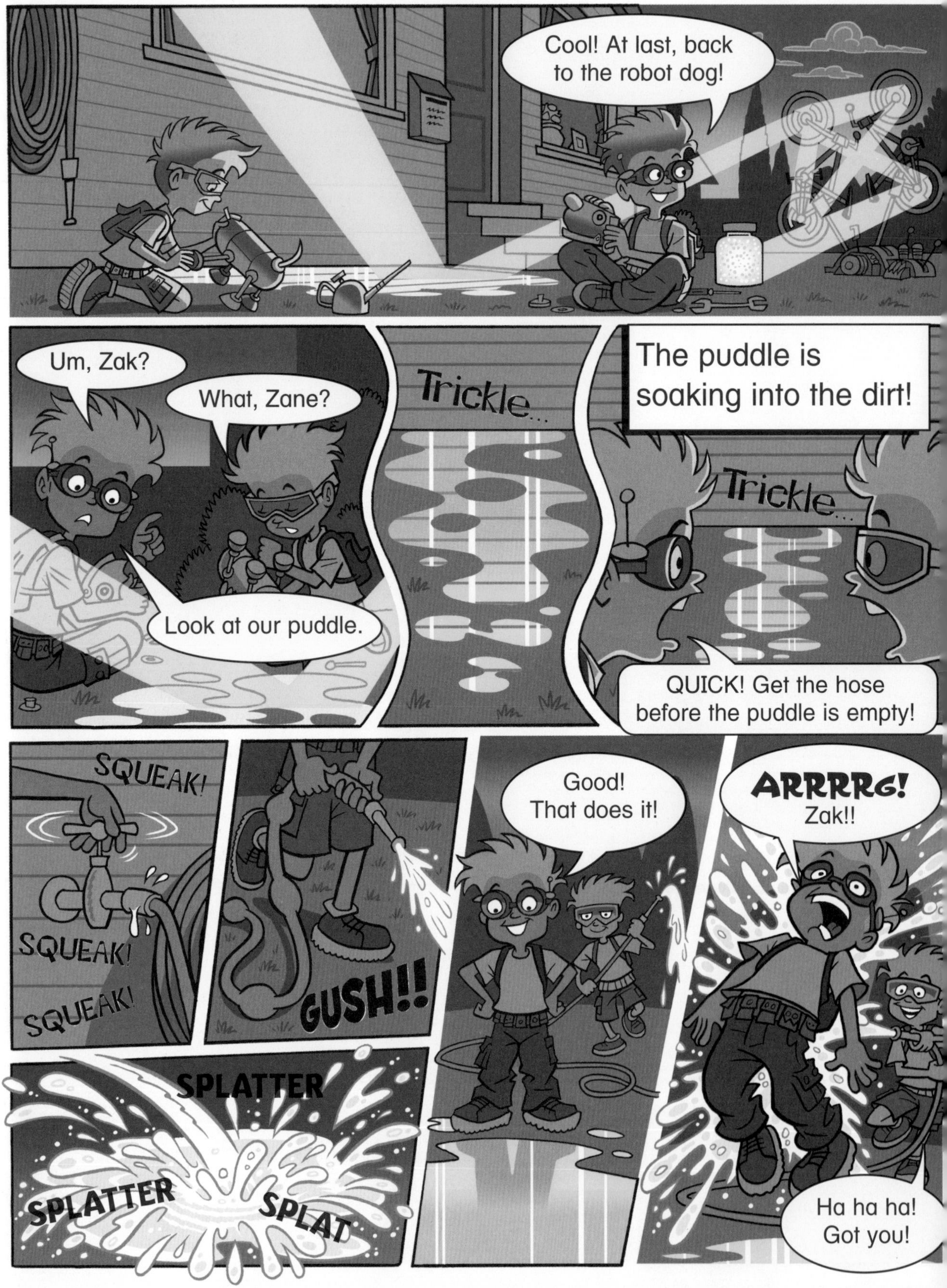
Cool! At last, back to the robot dog!
Um, Zak?
What, Zane?
Look at our puddle.
Trickle...
The puddle is soaking into the dirt!
Trickle...
QUICK! Get the hose before the puddle is empty!
SQUEAK!
SQUEAK!
SQUEAK!
GUSH!!
SPLATTER
SPLATTER
SPLAT
Good! That does it!
ARRRRG! Zak!!
Ha ha ha! Got you!

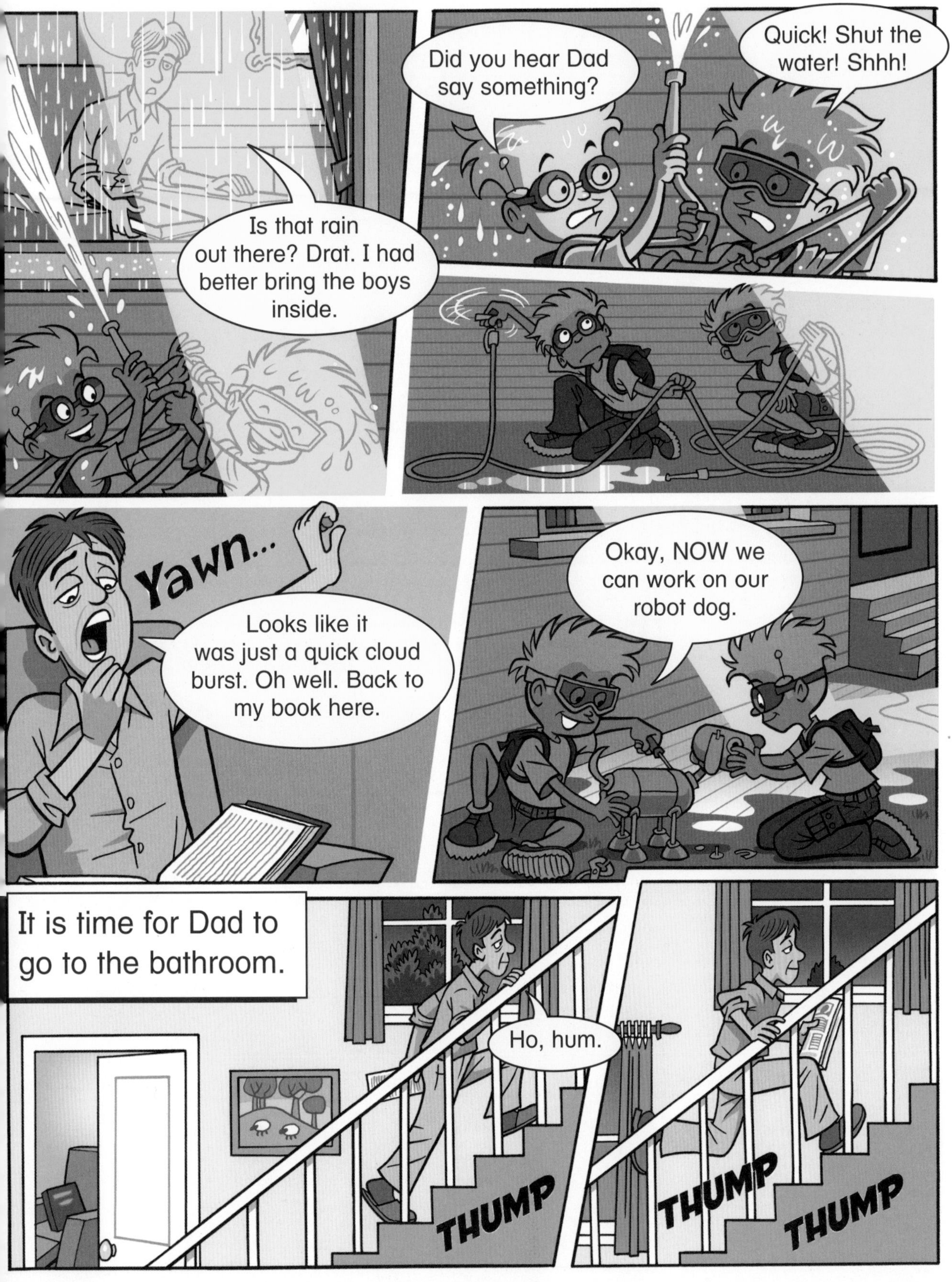
Is that rain out there? Drat. I had better bring the boys inside.
Did you hear Dad say something?
Quick! Shut the water! Shhh!
Yawn...
Looks like it was just a quick cloud burst. Oh well. Back to my book here.
Okay, NOW we can work on our robot dog.
It is time for Dad to go to the bathroom.
Ho, hum.
THUMP
THUMP
THUMP

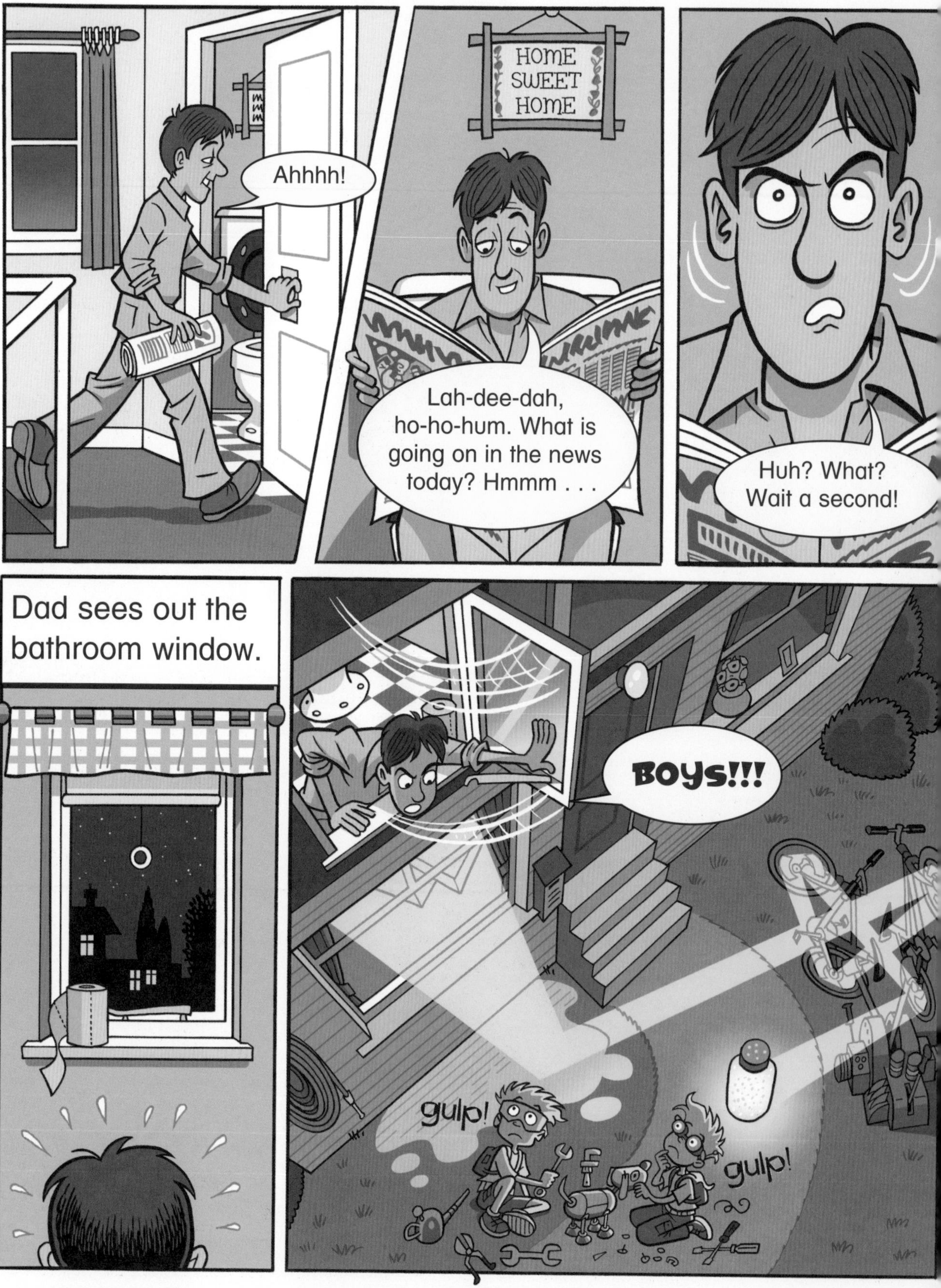
HOME SWEET HOME
Ahhhh!
Lah-dee-dah, ho-ho-hum. What is going on in the news today? Hmmm . . .
Huh? What? Wait a second!
Dad sees out the bathroom window.
BOYS!!!
gulp!
gulp!

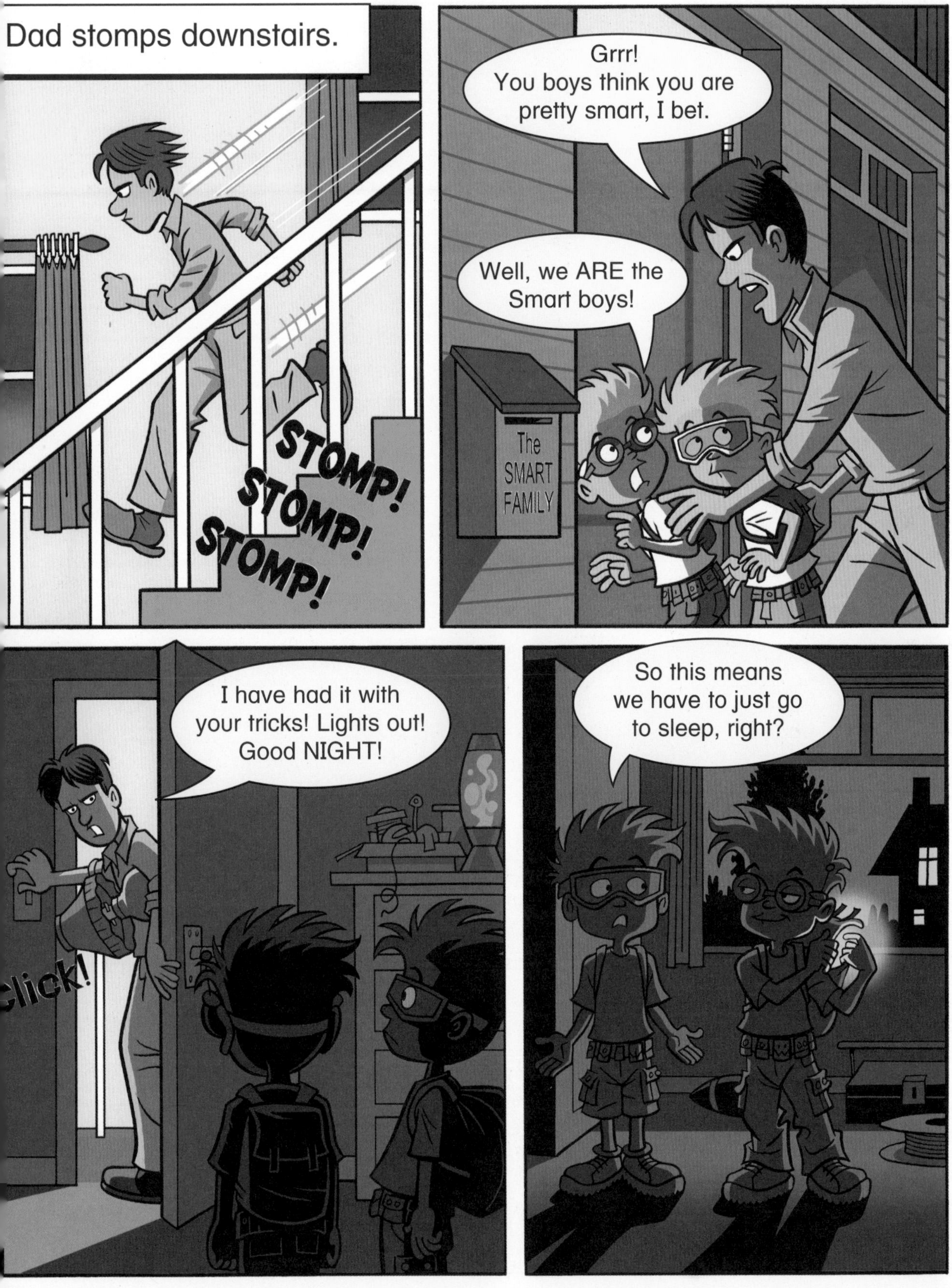
Dad stomps downstairs.
STOMP! STOMP! STOMP!
Grrr! You boys think you are pretty smart, I bet.
Well, we ARE the Smart boys!
The SMART FAMILY
I have had it with your tricks! Lights out! Good NIGHT!
Click!
So this means we have to just go to sleep, right?

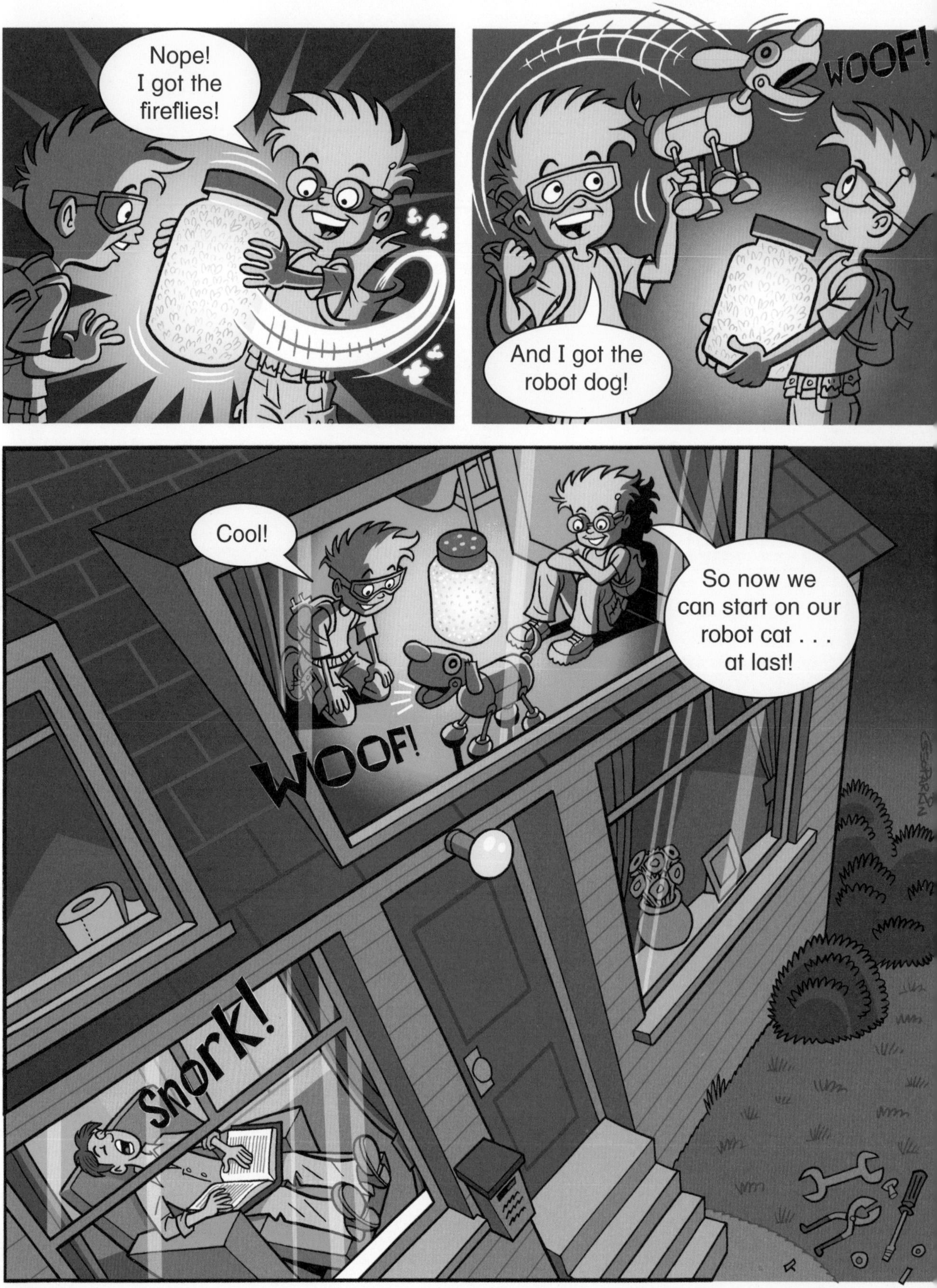
Nope!
I got the fireflies!
WOOF!
And I got the robot dog!
Cool!
So now we can start on our robot cat . . . at last!
WOOF!
Snork!